Edna O'Brien

The DAZZLE

British Library Cataloguing in Publication Data
O'Brien, Edna
  The dazzle.
  I. Title
  823'.914[J]   PZ7.O125/
  ISBN 0-340-26491-8

Text Copyright © 1981 Edna O'Brien
Illustrations Copyright © 1981 Hodder & Stoughton Ltd

First published 1981

Published by Hodder & Stoughton Children's Books
a division of Hodder & Stoughton Ltd,
Mill Road, Dunton Green, Sevenoaks, Kent TN13 2YJ

Designed by Graham Marks

Printed in Great Britain by Morrison & Gibb Limited, London & Edinburgh

Edna O'Brien
The DAZZLE

Illustrated by Peter Stevenson

HODDER AND STOUGHTON
LONDON SYDNEY AUCKLAND TORONTO

**E**VERY girl and every boy knows how hard it is to get to sleep. Either it's raining and the raindrops go pit-a-pat, pit-a-pat and then a big plop of it falls into the rain barrel OR it's windy and there's gales coming down the chimney OR there's a full moon and no matter how tight the curtains are drawn, one beam of light keeps shining in. If it's snowing any fool knows that there's a snowman outside in the garden, so lonely, with no one to talk to. As for thunder and lightning, that's the worst. Anything can happen. A bed, especially a bed on castors, can go all over the room. A tree can blow down. So can a chimney pot.

Tim knew all these hazards but there was something far worse. Every single thing in Tim's room spoke. How they spoke! How they blathered! How they got on his nerves! The trouble with them was that they only spoke when Tim was alone. Night after night, Tim could be heard saying, "Pipe down, picture; pipe down, Indian vase; pipe down, basin and jug," and sometimes he got so carried away that he shouted and his mother came up and would open the door and say, "Timothy!" Then all the items sang dumb and Tim had to close his eyes and let on that he was talking in his sleep.

"That boy has eaten too many crab-apples," his mother would say, and Timothy knew that next day he would get a pink powder crushed in a spoon of jam. A worm powder.

No sooner was she gone down the stairs than they were off again, yap, yap, yap. Tim would take his little silver torch from under the pillow and shine it on them and say, "Look at the mess you got me into," but no one pitied him. The curtain might give a shrug or the curtain rings start to laugh and make a tinkling sound like bracelets, but no one really cared. They were all too busy arguing and being ultra important. Another thing, they all wanted to be boss. Such arguments. The washbasin and jug argued as to who should hold the water. The jug said, "You hold this wretched water, it's far too heavy," and the basin replied, "Not till morning, silly, not till they wash him."

The toothbrush said, "I fancy toothpaste that tastes of raspberries or loganberries, my mouth is dry." The towel said, "Mooooooooooosh, mooooooooooosh." Tim liked the towel best because it meant no harm and was dopey. The towel craved for a bit of peace. But not the General in the big gold frame. He was obstreperous. He was a tall man with knee-high boots, a funny fur hat and a flashing sword. You could hear him in Timbuctoo. He was very cross and he would let out a big yell and cry, "Charge, man, charge!" He was either commanding infantry or cavalry. Sometimes his colour changed and he was like a beetroot. Tim thought 'I hope he doesn't get a fit or no one is safe.' "Pipe down, pipe down," Tim said, but in vain. Sometimes the General back-answered.

"Swine, swine," the General would say and Tim knew he meant trouble. Tim then took the precaution of ducking down under the blankets and pulling the big pink eiderdown up over his head until it was heaped like a sandcastle and he was buried under it. Of course, he couldn't stay there for long in case he smothered.

The most saucy one in the room was the Statue of the Infant. It knew everything. It knew secrets. It was stumpy and gold with a red mitre on its head and a golden staff in its hand.

"Timothy was a bad boy, today," it said, and then told how Tim had put two clods of mashed potatoes under the chair and later stole into the vestibule and picked out a glacé cherry from the top of the trifle. His mother put the trifle there to set because the vestibule had a tiled floor and was very cold. They had trifle on Sundays and they had steamed pudding every other day. The Infant statue knew the way Tim strove at a loose tooth and wobbled and wobbled it to make it fall out. Every time a tooth fell out Tim got a threepenny bit.

If Tim had one wish it would be to move the Statue, to put it out on the landing, or in the guest room. It was a menace the way it made his secrets public and called for him to be denounced. It was like a trial, the way each thing passed judgement on him. If they went too far, the mop said, "Out of order, out of order," because the mop was master. The mop had all the colours of the rainbow. When it swirled across the linoleum the dust just scattered, and in no time the floor would be very shiny and the dust shaken out of the window. However, the mop was divided into two. There was the feathery part and there was the handle. Now the handle was most incensed. It said that to be a mop was beneath it. It said it was meant for bigger and braver things. It belonged outdoors, it was from an oak tree, and it wasn't going to

spend its life picking up dirt and fluff and dead moths and dead bees. It sometimes banged the floor and called for attention and Tim felt that it was a very unhappy mop. The General hissed when the mop did that and said, "Scum, you are all scum," and then, so as to shut the mop up, the soldier started to give orders to his men.

It was then and only then that the orange flower bowl spoke up.

"Gentlemen . . . . . gentlemen . . . . . please." The orange bowl was the most ladylike of all. She was in the middle of the mantelshelf and she was bright orange and very stand-offish. She had come from India. When things got very bad she cried. She said, "What am I doing in this terrible climate when I am used to sunshine and flowers and yam-yam trees." She really was miserable. She shrieked when the soot fell down the chimney and she shivered when it rained and moaned when the damp patch over the chimney got damper. She said, "There'll be mushrooms here one day." They all thought she was a cry-wolf.

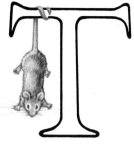**T**HEN one night a terrible wind began to blow and it poured with rain. They could hear the dog's plate rolling along the flagstones and the vase said, "This is it . . . doomsday." Next thing there was a groan as the bough of a tree cracked, and heaved and then fell down with a bang, and before he could say, "Crikey!", a huge drop fell on to Tim's nose and then another and then three in a row.

"Rescue, rescue!" Tim said.

"Who predicted this?" the orange bowl said.

"Sit tight," the basin said.

"Call the Reserves," the General said, and at that moment nearly a bucket of water fell on to Tim's face and fell into his eyes and made him miserable. He began to scream and after about twenty or thirty screams his mother and father came in. His father was carrying a candle but it was nearly quenched because of the wind.

The flame blew this way and that and was most feeble. Tim said, "I'm wet, I'm wet, I'm drenched," and his mother picked him up and wiped his face and said, "No, you're not, poppet." His father held the candle aloft so that they could see what had happened. Some of the wallpaper had peeled off the ceiling and was hanging down so that the rain dripped on to Tim's bed. His mother said how well it should happen just there and told his father to fetch the slop bucket. The green slop bucket looked really silly on Tim's bed. His father said they'd get Bob the builder to go up on the roof in the morning to put the slates back. He just hoped they hadn't broken.

"It was nasty," Tim said and scrunched his face. Now that they were nice to him, Tim thought he'd make the most of it and get a poached egg and cocoa. He was ravenous.

That night he slept in the big bed with his mother and
father. Was he snug! There were lovely, jazzy blankets,
several feather pillows and when he wanted to, he could
snuggle up next to his mother and then when he got too
hot, and started to perspire, he was able to move to the
edge of the bed. It was like being at the seaside, it was that
spacious. Tim thought, "I think I'll sleep here for the rest
of my life." In the morning they gave him breakfast in

bed. He had a big tray so it didn't matter if the cream rolled and spilt. His mother sat on the end of the bed and said did he want to play "I-spy"? He was never so happy in all his life. He was chuckling.

Then an awful thing happened. Tim's father came in and said, "The boy will have to go in the box-room." The job on the roof was much bigger and they would have to get scaffolding.

"Better get it ready," Tim's father said. Tim did not want to sleep in the box-room and said so.

"I don't like the box-room," he said and he scrunched his face up so's they'd know he was going to cry.

"There's no curtains in the box-room," Tim said, and now he was crying in earnest. His mother said they'd bring the flowered curtains from his room and put them up.

"I don't like the bed that's there," Tim said. "It wobbles." They said they'd move his own bed in. So it was a case of moving things, and making up the bed and Tim doing everything to let them know how unhappy he was, about the *whole* situation. He cried, then he sulked, then he refused his dinner and then he started gritting his teeth.

That night they made a very special exception and Tim was allowed to fall asleep on the armchair in front of the fire. There was all sorts of colours in the fire and they reminded Tim of the flags of each country. Green and gold flags, red and blue flags, yellow flags, and then . . . he went fast asleep.

TIM thought that he was still by the fire when he felt something pull his ear. He thought he was dreaming. No, he wasn't, he was in the box-room. The thing pulled a bit harder and Tim put his hand up and felt it. There on the pillow beside him was a Mouse, a very sleek Mouse.

"Who the dickens are you?" Tim said, and the Mouse replied, "I'm Mattie."

Tim said, "You've got a cheek; my mother puts traps down for the likes of you."

"Don't I know it," the Mouse said.

Tim thought that he was in a bit of a dilemma because if he was going to be nice to this Mouse he was bound to be in trouble with his mother.

"You won't squeal on me, Tim," begged the Mouse.

Tim thought, "He says my name very nicely, he can't be my enemy, or can he?" He had got very suspicious since the storm.

Then the mouse put a proposition to Tim. "Would you like to play a game that you've never played before?"

"Like what, smartie?" Tim thought, 'what sort of playing can you do in the dark, in a box-room, with a mouse? You can't throw stones or climb trees or bang things.'

"I'm tired," said Tim, "so buzz off." Tim flicked his hand and sent the Mouse careering off the pillow. The Mouse was now in the middle of the floor and all at once Tim saw a spot of light the size of a star, but much

brighter because it was in the room and not light years away in the heavens. Then the Mouse made a funny beep that must have been a code-beep because all of a sudden the star turned into a house that was like a crystal temple. Tim blinked at the beauty and brightness of the thing that stood in front of him. It shone like ice. An ice palace.

"Tell me what you want to see," the Mouse said very casually as if it was the most natural thing in the world. Tim was speechless. He did not know what to expect. Just then a squirrel appeared on top of a big tree, sticking its tongue out. It was a red squirrel.

"I can fly," said the Squirrel.

"No, you can't," said Tim, because he was jealous, because he'd always wanted to fly, and he was promised that when he grew up he could have a glider.

"Yes, he can," said the Mouse, "because, you see, he's my cousin."

The Squirrel flew from one branch to another and was showing off.

"I'll be blowed," Tim said.

"What else would you like to see?"

"I'd like to see a squid," Tim said. He was determined to think up something really difficult so he proposed a red squid that was gigantic and that was three trillion leagues under the sea. He had got out of bed in astonishment. There, right down in the depths of the sea was this great, grinning squid and not only that, but Tim could see the different colours of the sea, the blue on top, then the green and then the blue-black, leagues and leagues of it and the big squid yawning.

"What would you like him to do?" the Mouse asked.

"Eat, of course," said Tim. He wasn't going to let on how mesmerised he was.

"Eat what," said the Mouse.

"Eat a swordfish," said Tim.

"Why a swordfish?" asked the Mouse.

"Because it's tasty," said Tim, and at that second a silver swordfish flew into the squid's mouth and when the squid swallowed it there was a sound of bones getting mashed.

Then he saw his own climbing tree in his own kitchen garden, with a ladder leading up to it. On every step of the ladder there was a performing dog. There were mostly small, furry dogs and they were all black with white spots or white with black spots. They were spaniels.

They gave the paw, or danced, or did whatever
trick was required of them. They did it to music. They
disappeared at the crack of a whip. They were most
obedient. One of them went into Tim's tree-house and
brought out the bit of rope that was there and played with
it, and pretended to eat it as if it was shredded wheat.

The Mouse promised Tim that he could see anything
he liked. He only had to say the word and the Mouse
would do a little "abracadabra" and Bob's your uncle.

"How do you do it?" said Tim to the Mouse.

"It's my Dazzle," said the Mouse.

"Can you see anything you want?" said Tim.

"Anything," said the Mouse.

"Bet you can't see maggots," said Tim, joking.

"Bet you can," said the Mouse and Tim saw
all these maggots and he began to squirm.

"Can you see good things and bad things?" said Tim.

"Of course," said the Mouse.

Tim didn't know what the Mouse had up his sleeve. He thought that he was going to have lots of entertainment, but he was in for a shock.

The Mouse said, "Tim, prepare yourself, I'm warning you."

"For what?" said Tim.

"For danger," said the Mouse.

"Jeepers!" said Tim.

"For the worst thing that could ever happen to you," said the Mouse.

"Holy smoke," said Tim, and before he could jump back into bed or call for help, it began to happen.

WHAT do you think Tim saw? He saw his father dressed in his black dress suit with his black dicky bow, and stiff white collar. His father was in front of the mirror and he was putting his top hat on. His father was going out somewhere. Then he saw his father stretch his hand out and *then* he saw his mother. His mother was dressed like a fairy queen. She had a white dress with spangles on it and she had a cloak and her best handbag. *His mother and father were going out!* Tim was going to be all alone in the house. He saw them leave the kitchen, go down the hall and into the vestibule, and they went out. Tim heard the door bang. He knew he was all alone. He heard the pony and trap drawing up and then the jingle as they rode off, and he knew they were going down the long, long avenue to the gate. He was so scared he couldn't even cry. He was like jelly.

"I knew it was too good to be true," he said, and the Mouse said, "Just hang on, Tim."

"I can't," said Tim. "I'm afraid."

"What are you afraid of?" the Mouse asked.

The trouble was Tim was afraid of everything. He was afraid of the top step of the stair and the next step and the next. He was afraid of the well under the stairs and he was afraid of the hall and the big pair of antlers and he was afraid of the sitting room and the dining room and the breakfast room and the gun room and the kitchen and the back kitchen and the pantry and the cellar.

"What's there to be afraid of?" asked the Mouse, and

reminded Tim of his time in the other bedroom with all those lunatics yapping and talking and reprimanding him.

"That was different," said Tim.

"Why was that different?" said the Mouse. "That Statue was out to get you into trouble."

"But I was used to them," said Tim.

"Well, you'd better get used to the stairs and the antlers and the kitchen and the gun room . . . ," said the Mouse, "hadn't you?"

"Never!" said Tim. He said it with great determination.

"Let's explore," said the Mouse.

"I'm not able," said Tim. He was really afraid and his legs were shaking and he thought, 'I haven't even got my slippers.'

"Let's risk it," said the Mouse. "Let's trot down and meet some of these ogres."

"You'll come?" said Tim. If he had someone then he'd have a bodyguard!

"Of course," said the Mouse. "I'm itching to go."

"But it's spooky," said Tim.

"Not with my Dazzle," said the Mouse, and he started to push it towards the door. It was very mobile.

"We'll dazzle them," said the Mouse.

"All of them?" said Tim.

"Every single one of them," said the Mouse.

Tim wasn't so sure. He'd had one fright already and he didn't want another.

"But what'll we do when we get down there?" said Tim.

"Make ourselves at home," said the Mouse.

"How?" said Tim.

"We'll have a drop of brandy," said the Mouse.

"Brandy?" said Tim; that was a bit outrageous.

"From the big snifter," said the Mouse.

"You might fall in," said Tim. He was getting his courage back.

"You'll fish me out," said the Mouse. Then the Mouse said that they would have a cigar, and loll in front of the fire, relax, maybe open a tin of sardines. They'd stop at nothing!

"We'll tell everyone to go to hell," said the Mouse.

Tim thought, brave talk indeed, but what about Myrtle the cat. But before he even said it, the Mouse said, "Just one thing, Tim, Myrtle has got to be put out."

"Right you are," said Tim.

"Let's go," said the Mouse.

"Deffo," said Tim. He asked the Mouse if he could play with the piano accordion.

"You can play with anything you like," said the Mouse. "Hurry up, I'm peckish. I had no lunch, I was out in the fields all afternoon." So the Mouse was a field mouse *and* a house mouse. He was a very puzzling Mouse indeed.

"Peckish for what?" said Tim.

The Mouse said that, surprisingly enough, he did like cheese but he liked it fresh and crumbly and not that bit of dry, sweaty cheese that was put on traps.

"There's plenty of that," said Tim and he turned the door knob and felt very brave because at least he knew the run of the house and knew where they kept the key of the meat safe.

"Let's go, pal," Tim said, and no sooner had he said it than he heard his mother call.

"Tim, Timothy,"

He ran back to bed.

"You cheat, they've not gone out at all."

"I know," said the Mouse.

"So why did you play a trick on me?" asked Tim.

"To teach you," said the Mouse.

"Teach me what?" asked Tim, as if he hadn't enough boring lessons at school.

"You're not afraid now," said the Mouse.

Tim thought, 'that's true. I thought I was all alone and I wasn't afraid.' He thought, 'they can go out if they want.' He was quite looking forward to it. 'They could go to a hunt dance or a whist drive.'

"We've got the Dazzle," said the Mouse.

"Oy, oy," said Tim. They could hear his mother coming up.

"Don't squeak on me, Tim," said the Mouse.

"You're my pal," said Tim and he hopped into bed and shut his eyes.

When his mother stood over him with the candle, she thought that she had never seen Tim look so happy or so content.